RUDE ROGER
by TONY GARTH

Roger was a very rude little boy.

When his next door neighbour passed back his ball, Roger stuck out his tongue instead of saying "thank you".

"How rude!" said the neighbour, in disgust.

At school, the teacher asked Roger to hand out the books. But Roger just laughed. The teacher asked him again. This time, Roger shouted, "No, I won't!"

"Don't be so rude, Roger," said the teacher, and sent him to see the headmaster.

Roger got a good telling off. But he didn't care.

"Your nose looks like a turnip," Roger said to his headmaster.

He had to write out "I must not be rude to the headmaster" 100 times in his best handwriting.

At the supermarket, Roger helped his Mum pack up the shopping at the checkout.

"You're looking very smart today, Roger," the cashier said.

Roger blew a raspberry.

"Well, I never!" the cashier exclaimed. "How rude!"

Even at dinner time, Roger was rude. His table manners were awful.

He ate with his mouth open.

He stuffed his mouth full of potato and tried to speak.

He ate his peas with his knife.

He burped very loudly.

Roger's Mum and Dad didn't know what to do. He was getting ruder and ruder every day.

Then his Dad had a brilliant idea.

Next day, Roger's Dad took them all to the zoo. Roger was thrilled. He stuck out his tongue, rolled his eyes and made chicken noises at his Dad.

At the zoo, Roger met the zoo keeper.

"This is Mr Parks, Roger," said his Dad. "He takes care of all the animals."

"Hello," said Roger to Mr Parks. "You look like a monkey's bottom!"

Mr Parks took Roger to a table.

"You've been invited to tea with Eddie and Elsa," he said. "Now, you sit down. They'll be along in a minute."

"Who are Eddie and Elsa?" Roger asked his Mum and Dad.

They just smiled mysteriously.

"You'll see," said his Dad.

Roger sat down. The table was covered with cakes and sandwiches, trifle, jelly, and lots of fizzy pop! It was going to be a great tea.

To show his excitement, Roger blew a raspberry at his Mum.

"Don't be so rude, Roger," she said.

So Roger blew another!

Just then Mr Parks returned with Eddie and Elsa. They were chimpanzees!

"Now, Roger," said Mr Parks. "Can you look after these two and make sure they eat their tea?"

"Sure!" said Roger, and stuck out his tongue.

Eddie and Elsa climbed on to the table.

"Watch out!" said Roger. "You'll spill the pop."

But Eddie took no notice. He just blew a raspberry straight at Roger and kicked over all the drinks.

Elsa put her hands in the jelly and started throwing it at Roger.

"Hey! Don't do that!" Roger said, as a blob of jelly hit him.

Elsa just pulled a face and threw a bun at Roger.

"That's not very nice," Roger scolded.

But Eddie and Elsa didn't care.

Elsa jumped on Roger and started to pick through his hair.

"What are you doing?" he cried.

"I think she's looking for bugs," called Roger's Mum.

"Get off," yelled Roger. "I haven't got bugs!"

Then Mr Parks returned for the chimps.

"Time for bed," he said. "Say good night to Roger."

The chimps pulled a face instead.

"That was great," said Roger. "I really like chimps. But they'd be a lot nicer if they weren't so rude!"

"Some people say the same about you, Roger," said his Mum.

"Oh dear," said Roger. He thought for a while.

"From now on," he said, "I'll try not to be so rude. Because it isn't very nice."

"I'll start tomorrow," he added.

"Nyaaaa!!!!"

Look out for the next six Little Monsters!

HELPFUL HENRY

SHY SOPHIE

BOSSY BETHANY

REVOLTING RONNIE

WORRIED WINNIE

TV TREVOR

Cover printed Hexachrome, inner section printed 4 colour process by Speedprint (Leeds) Ltd. Tel: 0113 245 3665.